Clover the Bunny

For Rosa and Cynthia, the
guinea pigs — J.C.

Text copyright © 2016 by Jane Clarke and Oxford University Press
Illustrations copyright © 2016 by Oxford University Press

All rights reserved. Published by Scholastic Inc., 557 Broadway, New York. NY
10012, *Publishers since 1920*. SCHOLASTIC and associated logos are trademarks
and/or registered trademarks of Scholastic Inc. Published by arrangement
with Oxford University Press. Series created by Oxford University Press.

First published in the United Kingdom in 2015 by Oxford University Press,
Great Clarendon Street, Oxford, OX2 6DP.

The publisher does not have any control over and does not assume any
responsibility for author or third-party websites or their content.

No part of this publication may be reproduced, stored in a retrieval system,
or transmitted in any form or by any means, electronic, mechanical,
photocopying, recording, or otherwise, without written permission of the
publisher. For information regarding permission, write to Oxford University
Press, Attention: Rights Department, Great Clarendon Street, Oxford,
OX2 6DP, United Kingdom.

ISBN 978-0-545-87336-9

10 9 8 7   17 18 19 20

Printed in the U.S.A.   23
First edition, April 2016

Book design by Mary Claire Cruz

Clover the Bunny

Jane Clarke

Scholastic Inc.

Chapter One

Peanut peeked around the door of Dr. KittyCat's clinic.

A line of young, fluffy animals was waiting outside. They were all twisting and turning uncomfortably and scratching at their paws. Peanut slammed the door and turned tail into the room.

"Eek!" he squeaked. "There's an outbreak of pawpox in Thistletown!"

"Don't panic, Peanut," Dr. KittyCat meowed calmly. "Every doctor sees lots of cases of pawpox. Almost everyone catches it when they're young. Didn't you have it when you were a little mouse? It's very infectious."

"I did," Peanut squeaked. "It was horrible. My paws were so itchy I spent all day scratching, and I couldn't sleep!" His whiskers quivered. "I don't want to have it again."

"You can't get pawpox twice," Dr. KittyCat reassured him. "I caught it when I was a kitten—so neither of us will catch it again. We are both immune."

She buttoned up her white doctor's coat and swished her striped tail. "Now, who's first in line to see us today?"

Peanut scampered over to his desk and picked up Dr. KittyCat's *Furry First-aid Book*. The *Furry First-aid Book* was where they kept track of all their patients. Then Peanut went to open the door. A little black kitten crept into the clinic.

"Hello, Daisy," Peanut greeted her. "How can we help?"

Daisy blinked her big round eyes.

"I don't feel very well," the kitten snuffled. "My legs and tail ache."

"I'm sorry to hear that, but you've come to the right place," Peanut told her. "Dr. KittyCat's a fantastic doctor."

He glanced at Daisy's paws. "That's odd," he told Dr. KittyCat. "I don't see any spots."

"One of the first signs of pawpox is feeling unwell and achy," Dr. KittyCat murmured, "and the patient often has a mild fever. I need to take your temperature, Daisy."

Peanut clicked open Dr. KittyCat's flowery doctor's bag, took out the ear thermometer, and fitted it with a new hygiene cover.

He handed it to Dr. KittyCat and watched as she gently inserted it into Daisy's ear and waited for the *beep, beep, beep.*

Dr. KittyCat removed the thermometer and showed Peanut the reading.

"That's slightly above normal for a kitten," he squeaked. He threw away the hygiene cover and returned the ear thermometer to Dr. KittyCat's bag. Then he opened Dr. KittyCat's *Furry First-aid Book* and wrote down Daisy's temperature in it.

"Now, Daisy," Dr. KittyCat meowed, "let me take a closer look at your paws."

"I'll find the surgical head lamp . . ."
said Peanut, rummaging through a chest
of drawers. "Got it!"

He handed Dr. KittyCat what
looked like a little light on a headband.
Dr. KittyCat put it on and clicked on
the bright light. "You *are* a good kitten,"

she told Daisy as she examined each tiny paw in turn.

"I can see some small spots, Daisy," Dr. KittyCat meowed gently. "They're very faint at the moment, but they will get bigger, I'm afraid. You definitely have pawpox."

Daisy hung her head.

"Pawpox isn't a serious disease," Dr. KittyCat purred comfortingly. She handed Peanut the head lamp to put away. "But the spots will get itchy as they get bigger, and they may blister. Try not to scratch them."

"I remember how hard that is!" Peanut squeaked.

Dr. KittyCat reached up a paw and took a tube from the supply closet.

"This cooling gel will help soothe the itch," she told Daisy. "Go home and rest, and drink plenty of water. Pawpox doesn't make you feel sick for long," she ⌐ed the little kitten. "You'll soon r, and you'll never catch it

n

"You've been a very good patient," Peanut said as he opened the door for Daisy to go out. "I think you've earned one of our special reward stickers." He handed a round sticker that said: "I was a purr-fect patient for Dr. KittyCat!"

Daisy's eyes sparkled. "I feel a bit better already," she purred.

I was a purr-fect patient for Dr. KittyCat!

It had been an extremely busy morning.

"How many cases of pawpox did I treat?" Dr. KittyCat asked Peanut.

Peanut checked his notes.
"Fourteen!" he squeaked.

Dr. KittyCat washed her paws and
settled down in a chair with a sigh. She
took a ball of yarn out of her flowery
doctor's bag and began to click-clack
away with her knitting needles.

Peanut glanced up nervously from his desk. *Oh dear,* he thought, *that's a mouse-sized scarf . . . I hope it's not for me.* Peanut wasn't always very keen on Dr. KittyCat's hand-knitted things! His tail twitched as he took out his pencil and began to write up his notes in the *Furry First-aid Book.*

The old-fashioned telephone on the desk began to ring. Peanut and Dr. KittyCat exchanged glances.

Brring!
Brring!

Brring!
Brring!

15

It could be an emergency, Peanut thought as he grabbed the handset.

"Dr. KittyCat's clinic," he said. "How can we help you?" He listened for a moment, then put his paw over the mouthpiece.

"It's Pumpkin," he told Dr. KittyCat. "He's heard about the outbreak of pawpox and wants to know if we are going ahead with the camping trip later today." Peanut glanced down at his notebook. "Daisy; Posy, the puppy; and Fennel, the fox cub, all have pawpox, and Sage, the owlet, has clawpox." He sighed. "So they can't come. Do you think we should cancel it?"

Dr. KittyCat gazed thoughtfully out of the window. "Pumpkin, the hamster; Nutmeg, the guinea pig; and Clover, the bunny, are fine," she purred, "and the sun's shining. It would be a shame to cancel . . ."

"The camping trip's on!" Peanut squeaked into the phone's mouthpiece. "Tell the others to meet us outside the clinic. See you soon." He could hear Pumpkin squealing excitedly at the other end of the phone. Peanut smiled as he replaced the handset. The phone's curly cord wrapped itself around his furry little body.

"Eek!" he squeaked.

Dr. KittyCat put down her knitting and untangled him.

"Before we go, I need to check the medical supplies," she said, opening her flowery doctor's bag. "Scissors, syringe, medicines,

ointments, instant cold packs, paw-cleansing gel, and wipes," she murmured. "Stethoscope, thermometer, tweezers, bandages, gauze, reward stickers . . . and I think we should take the surgical head lamp and magnifying glass, too."

Peanut took them out of the drawer. "We'll be miles away from the clinic," he squeaked. "We should take some cooling gel in case someone comes down

with pawpox!" He
scrambled up
into the supply
closet, grabbed a box,
and dropped it into Dr. KittyCat's bag.

Dr. KittyCat squeezed her
knitting into the top of the bag
and clicked it shut.

"It's best to be prepared for
anything," she meowed. "We
should always be ready to
rescue!"

Chapter Two

Peanut looked up from his notes and glanced out the window. The vanbulance was parked right outside, and the bright flowers he had painted on it were sparkling in the sunshine. Pumpkin, Nutmeg, and Clover were standing next to it, jumping up and down with excitement. They were

each carrying a backpack and a
sleeping bag.

"They're here," Peanut squeaked.
He grabbed his pencil and the *Furry
First-aid Book* and went out to join the
little animals.

"I can't wait to see inside the
vanbulance," Clover said as he hopped
up and down while Peanut opened the
side door.

"Wow!" Nutmeg said excitedly.

"Wow-eee!" Pumpkin and Clover
exclaimed. "It's great!"

The little animals piled into the
vanbulance with their backpacks and
sleeping bags.

"It has a real table," Pumpkin squeaked, "and lots of cabinets."

"And a little kitchen with a kettle," Nutmeg whistled.

"And lovely polka-dotted curtains," Clover said. "But where will we all sleep?"

"This bench seat turns into Dr. KittyCat's bed," Peanut explained, "and that's my room up there." He pointed to a cabin just under the roof. "I've packed tents for you three to sleep in, and we'll all eat around the campfire. It's going to be an adventure!"

"Ooh!" The little animals squealed in excitement.

Peanut pointed to the bench seat.

"Hop up here and put on your seat belts. We'll be leaving in a minute," he told them.

Clover took a coloring book and crayons out of his backpack and put them on the table.

"We can color as we go along!" he said.

Nutmeg looked out the window. "Dr. KittyCat's coming," she squeaked.

"She's got her flowery doctor's bag with her."

"Good." Peanut laughed. "We can't go without that!" He checked that the animals' seat belts were pulled tight, then he shut the door and scampered around to the front of the vanbulance.

"Everyone's safely in the back," he called as he scrambled into the passenger seat. Dr. KittyCat opened the door to the driver's side of the vanbulance, threw her flowery doctor's bag onto the floor in front of Peanut, and jumped into the driver's seat.

Peanut clicked on his seat belt and carefully curled his tail out of the way before pulling the door shut. Dr. KittyCat did the same.

"Ready to roll?" Peanut squeaked.

"Ready to roll!" Nutmeg, Clover, and Pumpkin chorused from the back of the vanbulance.

Dr. KittyCat turned the key. There was a *vroom, vroom, vroom,* and the vanbulance sped off.

"Put the siren on!" Nutmeg whistled.

"We can't do that in town unless it's an emergency, and we're rushing to the rescue," Peanut explained. "And it isn't. Even though we are going really fast!" He glanced at Dr. KittyCat. Her bright eyes were fixed on the road ahead, and

she was smiling as she gripped the big
steering wheel tightly. The vanbulance
rattled over Timber Bridge and headed
toward Duckpond Bend.

Peanut shut his eyes. He could feel

the vanbulance tilt as they rounded the
corner.

"Ooh!" Nutmeg, Pumpkin, and
Clover squeaked.

Peanut opened his eyes as Dr.
KittyCat accelerated past the sports
field. In no time at all, they left
Thistletown behind.

The vanbulance bounced and
shook over the
potholes as
Dr. KittyCat
drove it along
the narrow,
twisting
country lanes.

Thank you for
visiting Thistletown.
See you again soon!

There was a groan from the back. "Ugh!"

"Pumpkin feels sick!" Nutmeg and Clover yelled.

"Stop!" Peanut squeaked.

There was a *screech!* as Dr. KittyCat put her paw on the brakes. As soon as the vanbulance shuddered to a halt, Peanut leaped out and rushed to open the side of the vanbulance. Pumpkin, Nutmeg, and Clover tumbled out. Pumpkin flopped onto the grass with his eyes shut tight, groaning.

Ugh!

"What's the matter?"
Peanut asked.

"I feel sick!" Pumpkin
moaned as Dr. KittyCat joined
them. "My head aches."

"Did you bump it?" Dr. KittyCat
asked him.

"No." Pumpkin groaned.

"It might be pawpox!" Peanut
whispered in Dr. KittyCat's ear.

"And it might not be," she
whispered back. "Don't panic, Peanut."
Dr. KittyCat turned to Pumpkin. "When
did your head start to ache?" she asked.

"When I was doing some coloring,"
Pumpkin whimpered.

"I noticed you turning a little green," Nutmeg whistled. "I think you're just carsick."

"You're right, Nutmeg," Dr. KittyCat told the little guinea pig. "You'd make a good doctor."

"Thank you!" Nutmeg said, looking proud.

"Poor Pumpkin," Dr. KittyCat said comfortingly. "Carsickness is really horrible. Lie still for a minute," she told him, "and it will pass."

Peanut jumped into the vanbulance and fetched a thermos of water.

Dr. KittyCat helped Pumpkin take little sips. She turned to Nutmeg and

Clover. "Are you two feeling OK?" she asked them.

They nodded their heads.

"I feel OK now, too," Pumpkin said.

"Then we'll get back in the vanbulance and continue our trip," Dr. KittyCat meowed. "I'll try to remember to go more slowly."

"I think you should shut your
eyes for the rest of the trip," Peanut
whispered in the hamster's furry ear.

"We're not far from the campsite
now," Dr. KittyCat reassured everyone
as they set off again.

There was a little squeak from the
backseat. "Dr. KittyCat . . ." Pumpkin
called.

Peanut exchanged a nervous glance with Dr. KittyCat. Was Pumpkin going to be sick?

"Can you put the siren on . . . *please?*" the hamster asked.

Peanut and Dr. KittyCat looked at each other and smiled. Dr. KittyCat nodded.

Nee-nah! Nee-nah! Nee-nah!

"Just for a second or two . . ." Peanut said. Then he slammed his paw down on the dashboard button that put on the flashing light and the noisy siren.

"Yay!" Pumpkin, Nutmeg, and Clover squealed.

At last, the vanbulance bumped through an open gate into a grassy campsite at the edge of some woods.

"We're here!" Dr. KittyCat meowed. She switched off the engine. She slid open the doors and everyone jumped out.

Peanut looked around. "There's a campfire pit!" he exclaimed, pointing to a circle of stones.

Nutmeg, Clover, and Pumpkin rushed to help Peanut heave three rolled-up tents out of the vanbulance. "Make sure you put them up at a safe distance from the fire pit," he told them.

The animals pulled out the tent poles.

"It's best to choose a flat piece of ground to pitch your tent on," Peanut told them. They all worked together to put up the tents. Then Peanut took out a wooden mallet and went around hammering in tent pegs.

"Can I try?" Nutmeg asked. Peanut reluctantly handed her the mallet.

"Be careful, we don't want any accidents," he murmured, but it was too late.

"Ow!" Nutmeg squealed, jumping up and down, shaking her paw in pain.

Chapter Three

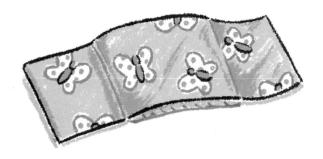

"Let me see," Dr. KittyCat said as she hurried over. Nutmeg held out her paw.

"It's just a tiny bruise," Dr. KittyCat said. "It doesn't even need a bandage."

Nutmeg's ears drooped.

"But it wouldn't hurt to have one," Peanut said, getting the box. Nutmeg grinned from ear to ear as she chose a bandage with butterflies on it. "Now, who wants to come with me to collect firewood?" Peanut asked.

"Me! Me! Me!" yelled Pumpkin, Nutmeg, and Clover.

Dr. KittyCat smiled. "You have plenty of helpers, Peanut," she purred. "I'll stay here. I have a surprise to get ready for everyone."

"What is it?" Peanut and the little animals squeaked.

"It wouldn't be a surprise if I told you!" Dr. KittyCat gave them a wave and headed toward the vanbulance.

"Stay together, everyone," Peanut

told Nutmeg, Clover, and Pumpkin as he led the way down the narrow path into the woods. "Don't wander off—you might get lost."

The air was cool and still in the woods. Bright green leaves were beginning to burst from the hazelnut and oak trees, and the ground was carpeted in a beautiful purple haze of bluebells. Peanut stopped in a grassy clearing.

"Dead wood makes the best firewood," he said. "And there are lots of fallen trees around here." He tugged at a dry branch attached to an old tree trunk. It came away in his paws with a loud *crack*!

"Ow!" Peanut exclaimed, shaking his paw. A sharp piece of wood was sticking out of it. It hurt a lot. It made his whiskers quiver.

Clover's eyes opened wide. "That's a big splinter!" he gasped.

"I'll get it out." Peanut gritted his teeth and pulled. But the end of the wood broke off, leaving the point buried in his paw.

"Let me look," Nutmeg said. She took Peanut's paw the way Dr. KittyCat had held hers and stared closely at it. "Oh dear," she whistled. "You'll have to get Dr. KittyCat to take that out."

Peanut knew she was right. "It shouldn't take long," Peanut told the other animals. "Don't leave the clearing. I'll be back in no time."

He scurried down the path,
cradling his hurt paw in his good one.

"Eek!" he cried as he reached the
vanbulance. "Dr. KittyCat, I need your
help! There's a splinter in my paw!"

Dr. KittyCat was blowing up a big
round pool with an air pump.

"They'll love that!" Peanut squeaked as Dr. KittyCat plugged the valve. "It's a great surprise."

"It is, isn't it?" Dr. KittyCat purred. "Let me treat your splinter and then you can help me fill the pool with water."

"I can't stay," Pumpkin squeaked. "I left Nutmeg, Pumpkin, and Clover in the woods. Please be quick!"

"Don't panic, Peanut," Dr. KittyCat said calmly. "It won't take long to get a splinter out. Go and wash your paw carefully in warm water, while I get my things ready." Peanut went to the little sink in the kitchen area of the vanbulance and soaped his paw under running water.

"Ouch!" he squeaked. "It's really painful."

Dr. KittyCat followed Peanut into the vanbulance and clicked open her flowery doctor's bag. She put on her surgical head lamp. "Let me see," she meowed.

Peanut put his paw into Dr. KittyCat's warm furry one. The splinter was so sore, his paw was shaking.

"It will stop hurting soon," Dr. KittyCat promised. "First, I'm going to take a look at the splinter to see how deep it is," she told Peanut. "Then I'll know the best way to get it out." Peanut held his breath as she carefully examined the site of the splinter.

"Good," Dr. KittyCat purred. "I can see the end of the splinter sticking up out of the skin, so I should be able to pull it out the way it went in." She reached for her tweezers. Peanut shut his eyes.

"There!" Dr. KittyCat told him. "It's out."

Peanut's whiskers stopped quivering. Dr. KittyCat was such a fantastic doctor, he hadn't even felt her removing the splinter.

"Gently wash the wound again and pat it dry," Dr. KittyCat told him. "Then I'll put a bandage over it to keep it clean."

Peanut did as he was told. He chose a bandage covered in little paw prints.

"It's almost as good as new," he said, admiring his clean pink paw with the bandage on it. He felt much better.

"Keep it clean and tell me if there's any increased soreness, redness, itching, or swelling," Dr. KittyCat said as she packed away her head lamp and tweezers. "You were very brave, Peanut," she purred.

Peanut felt as if he would burst with pride. Then he remembered . . . Pumpkin, Nutmeg, and Clover were waiting for him.

"I have to get back to the woods!" Peanut jumped out of the vanbulance and rushed toward the woods. What looked like two walking bundles of twigs were heading up the path.

Nutmeg and Pumpkin were carrying armfuls of firewood.

"We got lots of wood." Nutmeg panted from behind a pile of twigs.

"Great!" Peanut exclaimed. "But where's Clover?"

"He's not far behind us," Pumpkin said.

Peanut stared down the narrow path that led into the woods.

"I can't see him," he murmured.

"Waah!" A distant, shrill shriek echoed out of the woods. "Waah! Waah!"

Peanut raced back to Dr. KittyCat. "It's Clover. He's hurt!" he squeaked. "Ready to rescue?"

Dr. KittyCat picked up her flowery doctor's bag. "Ready to rescue!" she meowed. "We'll be there in a whisker!"

Chapter Four

Peanut grabbed the *Furry First-aid Book* and dashed down the path after Dr. KittyCat. Nutmeg and Pumpkin dropped their firewood and followed, too.

"Clover!" they all yelled. Peanut listened. Somewhere in the distance he thought he could hear a little animal sobbing. He held his breath. The grassy clearing in the woods was still and silent.

Nutmeg pointed at the entrance to a burrow. "What if Clover's hurt and he's crawled down a rabbit hole?"

"Clover!" they called. "Where are you?"

"Waah!" The little bunny's distress call seemed to echo all around them.

"It doesn't sound as if he's down a hole," Peanut said. "He's over there somewhere."

He pointed to the edge of the clearing. "Come on!"

Dr. KittyCat, Nutmeg, Pumpkin, and Peanut raced toward Clover's cries. At the far side of the clearing, there was a pile of wood near the base of an old tree trunk.

"He dropped his firewood," Pumpkin said, worried. "Something must have happened to him!"

"Waah!" Clover wailed again. Dr. KittyCat's ears pricked up. Peanut glanced around wildly, but all he could see was shadows.

"I've spotted him!" Dr. KittyCat exclaimed. She pointed to a little mound of fur huddled up in the dappled light. It was Clover,

quivering from his whiskery nose to his cotton tail.

"Waah!" Clover cried. "Waah!"

"Dr. KittyCat's come to rescue you, Clover," Peanut squeaked. "Everything will be all right now."

Dr. KittyCat knelt down beside the distressed bunny.

"What's wrong, Clover?" she asked him gently.

"My paws hurt!" the bunny sobbed.

"Did you fall over anything?" Dr. KittyCat asked.

"No!" Clover snuffled.

"Did a branch or anything hit you on the paws—or the head?"

"No!" Clover cried.

"That's good," Dr. KittyCat meowed reassuringly. "Can you wriggle all your paws?"

"Yes!" Clover whimpered.

"Good," Dr. KittyCat said again. She turned to Peanut. "Clover hasn't broken anything," Dr. KittyCat told him. "I think it's safe to move him."

"He's been collecting firewood. Maybe he's got splinters in his paw, like me," Peanut squeaked. "Splinters are very painful."

Nutmeg and Pumpkin nodded.

"I need to see your paws properly, Clover," Dr. KittyCat purred. "Let's move you out into the sunshine."

Clover nodded miserably as Dr. KittyCat and Peanut helped him to his feet.

"Ow!" he wailed.

Dr. KittyCat examined each of his paws.

"You don't have any splinters that I can see," Dr. KittyCat told Clover. "But you do have a rash all over your paw pads that are turning into blisters. The rash is worse on your back paws than on your front paws. It must be very sore and itchy."

"It is!" Clover wailed.

"Blisters?" Peanut opened Dr. KittyCat's *Furry First-aid Book* and leafed through the reference section.

"Eek!" He squeaked. "It's pawpox. Clover's caught pawpox! We will all have to pack up and go home!"

Nutmeg and Pumpkin looked at each other and burst into tears. "No!" they cried.

Chapter Five

"Don't panic, Peanut," Dr. KittyCat meowed. "It does look as if it might be pawpox, but I need to do a few more checks to make sure."

She turned to the little bunny. "Do you have a headache, Clover?" she asked.

Clover shook his head.

"Good," Dr. KittyCat murmured. "Do you have any other aches and pains?"

"Only in my paws," Clover moaned.

Dr. KittyCat turned to Peanut. "I need to check Clover's temperature," she told him.

Peanut opened Dr. KittyCat's flowery doctor's bag and passed her the ear thermometer. Dr. KittyCat gently placed it in Clover's ear and waited for the *beep, beep, beep* before taking it out.

"Clover doesn't have a fever," Dr. KittyCat said slowly, showing Peanut the display on the thermometer. "He might not have pawpox after all."

"I really hope he doesn't," Nutmeg whistled.

"Me too," agreed Pumpkin.

Peanut put the thermometer back into Dr. KittyCat's bag. "What's wrong with Clover's paws then?" he asked.

"They hurt!" the bunny squealed.

"Don't worry, Clover, we will find out what the problem is," Dr. KittyCat meowed. "What were you doing when your paws began to hurt?"

"Collecting firewood," Clover said between sniffs. "I got lots!" He nodded toward the big pile of dry sticks. "I was carrying it back to camp. But my paws hurt so much I had to drop it."

"Maybe he has lots and lots of tiny splinters," Peanut squeaked. He rummaged through her bag and handed Dr. KittyCat her surgical head lamp. "Would it help to use a magnifying glass?"

"Good idea!" Dr. KittyCat meowed. "Can you hold it steady for me?"

"I'll try, but my paw's still a little sore." Peanut carefully heaved the big heavy magnifying glass out from the bottom of Dr. KittyCat's bag. He clutched it in both paws and tried not to let it wobble, as Dr. KittyCat shone her head lamp on Clover's back foot and slowly examined each of the bunny's little paw pads.

"I can't see any splinters," she told Clover. She raised her head. "Thanks, Peanut, you've been a big help. You can put the magnifying glass down now."

"Whew." Peanut sighed with relief as he stashed the magnifying glass and the head lamp back in the bag.

"Close up, Clover's blisters look like clusters of wasp or bee stings, but much, much smaller," Dr. KittyCat told him.

A whole rash of teeny-tiny stings, thought Peanut. "Did you stomp on an ants' nest, Clover?" he asked.

"I don't think so." Clover snuffled.

"It's a bit of a puzzle," Dr. KittyCat

said, "but we will figure it out. Where were you gathering firewood, Clover?"

"Over there . . ." Clover waved a paw behind him toward a patch of dark green plants that were growing among the bluebells. A bunny-sized trail of flattened leaves led through them.

Peanut scampered over to take a look. The plants were higher than his head. They had leaves with raggedy edges and, from underneath, it looked as if they were covered in tiny hairs.

"I've got it! It's not pawpox!" Peanut squeaked. "We can stay and have our campfire after all!"

Nutmeg and Pumpkin jumped up and down squealing, "Yay!"

"So what *is* wrong with Clover?" Nutmeg asked after a few moments.

"He's been stung!" Peanut squeaked. "Clover has walked through a patch of stinging nettles!"

Chapter Six

"I didn't realize that I'd stepped in stinging nettles," Clover said.

"That's because you were carrying so much firewood," Nutmeg told him. "I couldn't see where I was going, either!"

"Poor Clover—nettle stings are no fun. No wonder your paws are so sore," Dr. KittyCat meowed. "Luckily, I

have something that will relieve
the pain."

She took out a tube of gel and
smoothed it on Clover's blistery rash.

Clover sighed with relief. "That
feels nice and cool," he said.

"The sting will slowly fade away,"
Dr. KittyCat promised.

"It's fading a bit already." Clover smiled a wobbly smile.

I was a purr-fect patient for Dr. KittyCat!

"You are a very brave bunny," Dr. KittyCat purred. "I have one of my special reward stickers for you in my bag."

"Thanks!" Clover's eyes lit up as Dr. KittyCat patted the sticker onto the little bunny's sweater.

"Can I have one?" Nutmeg whistled. "*Please?* I bruised my paw and you looked at it."

"And me!" Pumpkin squeaked. "I was carsick!"

Peanut glanced at his sore paw. "I had a nasty splinter," he squeaked. "Please, may I have a sticker, too?"

"Of course!" Dr. KittyCat smiled as they all stuck their stickers on. "Now, let's take the firewood back to the campsite," she meowed. "My surprise is waiting, and I need some help to fill it up."

"A pool! Yay!" The little animals squealed in surprise and excitement when they saw it. But Dr. KittyCat's striped tail drooped.

"Oh no!" she meowed. "It's gone down! It must have a leak."

"Don't panic, Dr. KittyCat!" Peanut
told her. "It's nothing that a mouse and
a box of bandages can't fix!"

He checked the pool over carefully.

"It has a splinter, too," he said,
pulling out a piece of sharp wood.

Nutmeg, Pumpkin, and Clover
heaped up the firewood in the campfire

pit while Peanut stuck bandages over
the hole in the pool. Dr. KittyCat
used the air pump to blow it up again.

"It's as good as new," she declared.

They all took turns filling it with
buckets of water from the campsite tap.
Then Peanut and the little animals
jumped in.

Splash!

"This is making
my paws feel much
better!" Clover
laughed as he and
his friends splashed
in the cool, refreshing
water.

Soon, it was time to dry off their paws and light the campfire. Peanut carried two folding chairs from the vanbulance, and Dr. KittyCat settled into one and took out her knitting.

"I've almost finished this scarf," she purred.

"Who's it for?" Peanut squeaked nervously.

"I haven't decided yet," Dr. KittyCat meowed. Flames crackled as they all joined in and sang campfire songs. As darkness fell, the fire died away to just a glow.

Peanut went back into the vanbulance and found a packet of marshmallows to toast. Nutmeg, Clover, and Pumpkin rushed to find sticks to thread them onto.

"Be careful—don't burn yourselves," he begged as the little animals held their marshmallow sticks over the remains of the fire.

"Yum!" Nutmeg whistled.

"Yummy!" Clover and Pumpkin agreed.

Dr. KittyCat finished the last stitch on the scarf she was making and popped it into her flowery doctor's bag. "Clover's already forgotten

about his nettle stings," she meowed.
"Look at him—he's covered in sticky
marshmallow from nose to toes!"

"And Pumpkin's forgotten all about
being carsick, and Nutmeg's forgotten
about hitting her paw." Peanut laughed.
"They're all having a wonderful time!"

"Everything's purr-fect
now!" Dr. KittyCat agreed.

There was a sudden loud yelp, and Nutmeg leaped to her feet.

"Something bit me!" Nutmeg whistled.

"And me!" Pumpkin yelled.

"And me!" Clover glanced wildly around him. "We're sitting on an ants' nest!" he squealed.

The little animals formed a line to see Dr. KittyCat.

"This cooling gel is very useful," Dr. KittyCat meowed as she treated the ant bites and gave out more stickers.

"Your stickers make everyone feel better, too." Peanut laughed.

"Bedtime!" Dr. KittyCat yawned as she closed her flowery doctor's bag. Clover, Nutmeg, and Pumpkin hopped off happily to their tents.

Peanut got a bucket and poured water from the pool over the glowing twigs until the hissing stopped, and the campfire was safely out. Then he went from tent to tent, listening to the rumbling sounds of small animal snores.

"They're all fast asleep," he confirmed.

Dr. KittyCat opened the door to the vanbulance. Peanut scampered up into his little cabin as Dr. KittyCat unfolded her bed.

"That was a very eventful day," she meowed, snuggling under her quilt. "I was thinking we could have a treasure hunt tomorrow."

"Great idea!" said Peanut sleepily. "As long as it doesn't involve going through any nettle patches or ants' nests! Good night, Dr. KittyCat!"

"Good night, Peanut!" Dr. KittyCat yawned. She was ready for a good night's sleep!

The end

What's in Dr. KittyCat's bag?

Here are just some of the things that Dr. KittyCat always carries in her flowery doctor's bag.

Surgical head lamp

Dr. KittyCat's surgical head lamp is battery-powered so that she can take it anywhere. She wears it on her head and is able to direct the bright adjustable spotlight to examine even the smallest cut, wound, or rash.

Ear thermometer

Dr. KittyCat uses her ear thermometer to see if a patient has a higher than normal temperature. This is called a fever. She knows when to look at the reading because the thermometer makes a beeping sound when it's ready.

Tweezers

Dr. KittyCat finds tweezers very handy for removing splinters, but she also uses them for cleaning grazes or cuts by carefully removing specks of dirt from the wound. Dr. KittyCat sterilizes her tweezers after each time she uses them.

Cleansing wipes

Cleansing wipes are individually wrapped and are moistened with sterile water. They are a very gentle way of washing an area to prevent the spread of germs. They do not contain any perfumes or chemicals that might irritate the skin of Dr. KittyCat's patients.

Dr. KittyCat is ready to rescue:
Posy the Puppy

Posy the **Puppy**

"I'll go in and keep her calm while we both figure out the best way to treat her and get her out," Peanut suggested.

"Good idea," said Dr. KittyCat. "Take a cold pack with you." She opened her flowery doctor's bag.

"Oooh!" The curious crowd pushed forward to get a better look.

Peanut scurried into the tunnel.

There was just enough sunlight shining through the tough canvas for him to make out a bundle of quivering golden fur. The fluffy little puppy was curled up in a tight ball in the gloom.

"I'm here now, Posy," he murmured.

A rubbery nose poked out of the fur ball. "Ow!" she yelped.

Don't panic, Peanut!

A note from the author:

Jane says . . .

"Our rabbit, Matilda, loved to dig burrows in her run in the garden she shared with guinea pigs, Rosa and Cynthia. One day, we couldn't find Cynthia. She was stuck down inside Matilda's burrow and needed rescuing. We had to dig her out!"

See you next time!

Visit Friendship Forest, where animals can talk and magic exists!

Meet best friends Jess and Lily and their adorable animal pals in this enchanting new series from the creator of Rainbow Magic!

SCHOLASTIC

scholastic.com

MAGICAF1